Good Touch- Bad Touch

Story – Kunal and Vedika

Illustrations – Creative Knot

This book belongs to:

_____

The summer vacation was unfortunately over, and it was time to go back to school. Sandra and Reema came to school after the two-month break, and they both had lots to share with each other.

"I went to my uncle and aunt's house. We stayed there for a month, and it was fun. My uncle took great care of me, and we played many games," Sandra said, jumping with joy.

Reema was not so cheerful. "We also visited a distant relative for a few days—an aunt and uncle of mine. My uncle also played with me, but his games were a bit strange." Reema felt uncomfortable explaining the exact nature of the games.

"My uncle and aunt gave me many moral storybooks, and we read them together," Sandra mentioned with a twinkle in her eyes. "My uncle offered me a seat near his chair while reading the stories. I really enjoyed it," Sandra continued.

"My uncle was not very fond of storybooks, but he made me watch movies with him. He explained them to me and also said that I am growing up and should see such movies, although sometimes it was very uncomfortable," Reema confessed.

"He often made me sit on his lap. I felt annoyed, but I think it was just his way of showing love and care," Reema explained with many pauses.

"I learned how to narrate stories with correct pronunciation there. My uncle and aunt would often ask me to read a book and whenever I would narrate the complete story correctly, my uncle would pat my head. I really liked it," Sandra stated proudly.

"That is really nice. My uncle also appreciated me many times, but he used to pat me on the lower back and sometimes on my buttocks as well," Reema said unhappily.

"Hey, I also learned football this time. My uncle called me to play whenever his son was playing. We did several other outdoor activities as well," Sandra informed happily about her new skills in football and other outdoor sports.

"That sounds like so much fun! But my uncle only called me for games when my mother and aunt were out. He asked me not to discuss his games with anyone else, saying they were private friend games between him and me," Reema explained.

It was clear from Reema's expression that she did not like his games.

"Anyway, leave it. What all outdoor activities did you do?" Reema asked to divert the topic.

"I played football, bat-ball, hide and seek, dog and bone, catch me if you can, and many other games along with my uncle and his son. Whenever I won any game, everybody clapped and uncle gave me my favorite chocolate. I loved it," Sandra cheerfully narrated the memory.

"My uncle also gave me a chocolate every day but asked me not to tell anyone, as my mother might object. I took it but now I feel I should have declined, as mother should know if we are taking something from someone," Reema disclosed.

"We also went fishing with the whole family and had lots of fun. While fishing, water got spilled on my uncle. He searched for a place to change his clothes for five minutes. He was very shy," Sandra giggled.

"My uncle was quite frank with me. He used to change his clothes in front of me and often asked me to change clothes there as well. He told me that we are friends, and it's okay to change in front of each other," Reema said, visibly upset.

Sandra paused. "Reema, I think your uncle was not good. Have you talked to your mom? My mother told me that we should not change our clothes in front of others."

"I thought he was a good person, but now I am confused. What should I do?" Reema asked, looking worried.

"Come, let's talk with our teacher." Sandra pulled Reema to the teacher's room.

Reema discussed her uncle's behavior with the teacher. The teacher made her comfortable and explained, "Reema, your uncle looks like a bad person. His behavior was inappropriate."

"How do we know about good or bad conduct, teacher?" Sandra asked.

A good touch of appreciation is a reward. It should be on the upper back or the head.

Any intentional touch to the chest, hips, or private parts, is bad. It must be objected to and reported to parents.

A game played in a group is good.

Asking for a secretive game is a bad demand, a bad conduct.

A children's story or cartoon movie is good.

Watching a movie with adult content is a bad conduct.

Offering a seat nearby is a good gesture.

One must not insist on making you sit on his lap.

Clothes should be changed alone in a separate room.

Changing clothes in front of a person of the opposite gender is not okay.

The teacher placed her hand on Reema's shoulder and said, "My dear, you must tell your parents about your uncle. Secretive games and touches that make you uncomfortable are red flags. Your safety and well-being are the top priority. It's important to speak up and remember that it's always okay to say 'No.'"

Reema felt relieved. "I will definitely talk to my parents about my uncle. Thank you so much, teacher."

FIND 5 DIFFERENCES

LEAVE A REVIEW

Dear Parents,

Thank you for choosing Good Touch-Bad Touch book. We believe the book has provided valuable insights and fostered important conversations about personal boundaries and body safety.

If you found the story engaging and educational, we would be thrilled if you could share your thoughts by leaving a review. Your feedback not only helps us improve but also guides other readers and parents seeking valuable resources on this vital subject.

Your support means the world to us!

With Love,
Kunal and Vedika

ABOUT THE AUTHORS

Dr. Kunal Das is a pediatric oncologist and stem cell transplant physician by profession. His art of telling stories inspired the compilation of stories in Doon Tales. He is a patient listener and an avid writer. He penned down many stories for children and enjoys writing novels in Hindi as well. He can explain any topic in interesting narratives and has the art of engaging children in that subject. Apart from writing skills, he is a good painter, a good orator, and an excellent professional in his field.

Dr. Vedika Agrawal is an engineering doctorate with an inclination towards children's literature. With a good understanding of kids' way of learning, she has written several children storybooks. She co-founded the publishing house, Doon Tales with an aim to imbibe reading habits and values in children through the magic of books. Other than writing, she likes playing sports.

MESSAGE FROM THE AUTHORS

Your body belongs to you. You can say 'No' if you don't want to be hugged or kissed by someone. If you feel scared or uncomfortable because of anyone's touch, you must talk to your parents or teacher about it.

About Doon Tales

Doon Tales provides a wide variety of storybooks ranging from stories focused on fun and adventure to those based on values and education. It is an initiative by Dr. Kunal Das (MD, FNB – pediatric oncologist, India) and Dr. Vedika Agrawal (Ph.D., IIT Delhi, India) to imbibe reading habit and values in children.

This book, Good Touch - Bad Touch is part of 'Let's Learn' series. 'Let's Learn' stories aim to help kids differentiate between the good and the bad, become responsible citizens, and lead a happy healthy life.

Other Titles in Let's Learn Series:

My Pandemic Diary
Limit Your Screen Time
My Little Sister
Nano's Visit to Dehradun
The Mystery of Alien Thief
Children Against Tobacco Menace

Books by Doon Tales - Let's Learn Picture Books

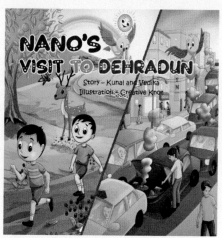

Books by Doon Tales - Animal Kingdom Picture Books

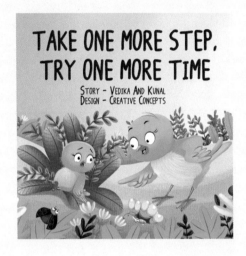

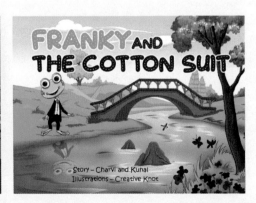

Books by Doon Tales - Moral Stories Picture Books

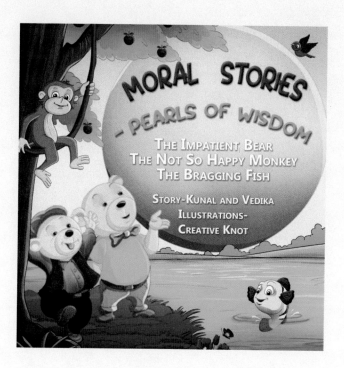

14482432R00019